BEANS

BEANS

Maddie Frost

WOMBATS!

Go Camping

VIKING

VIKING
An imprint of Penguin Random House LLC, New York

First published in the United States of America by Viking,
an imprint of Penguin Random House LLC, 2023

Visit us online at penguinrandomhouse.com.

Library of Congress Cataloging-in-Publication Data is available.

Manufactured in China

ISBN 9780593465295

10 9 8 7 6 5 4 3 2 1

TOPL

Book design by Maddie Frost
Typeset in Delivery Note and Lets Draw Fun Animals Bold
The illustrations in this book were created with Procreate.

To Toby.
It's always an adventure
with you, best friend.

RING-RING
MAIL

RING-RING
PICKLES
TO PACK
map
water
compass
tents

Mornin', Pickles! You ready to go?
TO PACK
map
water
compass
tents
A

Mornin', Bert, Buddy.
This is going to be the best day EVER!

You have all your essentials?

Yep!
BOING
1 MILLION PIECES

Did you pack light?

Oh yeah.

I can't wait to go swimming.
THE GREAT INDOORS
LUXURY CABINS

And eat by the fire.
SLURP

And relax under the stars.
THE GREAT INDOORS
LUXURY CABINS

SPLAT
BEANS
You're gonna love it.

Albert, guess what?
What?

I'M READY!

I thought you said you packed light?
I did.
MAIL

Party light!

Where's the rest of your stuff?

This is all my stuff.
Don't worry, you can get whatever you forgot at the shopping center.
Shopping center? There's no shopping center in the--
OH MY GOSH I FORGOT SOMETHING!

MAIL

Yummy, yummy pickles,
I love you.

Yummy, yummy pickles,
you know it's true.
BOOP

Yummy, yummy pickles,
you are my favorite
foo-ooo-ood.

Do you really need
the whole jar?

Albert! Yes.
And they can hear you.

See ya later, Platters! We're going camping. Bring you back a souvenir!

I don't think she's home. Look.
GONE FOR A STAKEOUT -P
GONE FOR A STAKEOUT -P
Gone for a stakeout? I thought she was a vegetarian?
Pickles, a stakeout doesn't mean-- Never mind, let's go.

So are we heading to the bus stop now?
WOODSY FOREST
CAMPGROUND
MAP OF WFC

There's no bus stop to the campsite, Pickles.

We'll get there with a map.

And we'll use a compass.

The red needle always points north. So since we want to go east, we line the needle up with the N and go in the direction of E.
N
W
E
S

Oh yeah.
I see what you're sayin'.

?

CAMP-SITES
Now let's put our best foot forward and hop to it.
Which foot is my best foot?

CRAM

We made it.
SITE #6

We made it!
Luxury cabin, I have arrived!

Where's the luxury cabin?
BUS SCHEDULE
INDOOR POOL
FITNESS CENTER
SPA SERVICES
SHOPPING CENTER
THE GREAT INDOORS

Luxury cabin?
Yeah, in this pamplet it says there's a luxury cabin.

Why do you have a brochure for luxury cabins at a resort called the Great Indoors?
You said we were going camping.

Haven't you ever been camping before?
Yes. Maybe... It's just...
I thought there was going to be an indoor pool.
And a big cozy chair by the fireplace.
AND A JACUZZI UNDER THE STARS!

I even brought my snazzy bathing suit!

Oops.

Oh, Pickles, that's not camping. That's glamping.
Camping is all about enjoying the outdoors.
BZZZZZZZZ

Embracing nature...
SMACK

Taking in the sights and smells...
yay poop!

And relaxing.
RIB-BURRRP
Don't you feel relaxed?

I feel...

POP

Deflated.
PFFFFFF

Let's set up the tents to make you feel more comfortable.

Just follow the steps in the directions.

It's pretty simple...

Let me know if you need help.

WHISTLE
WHISTLE

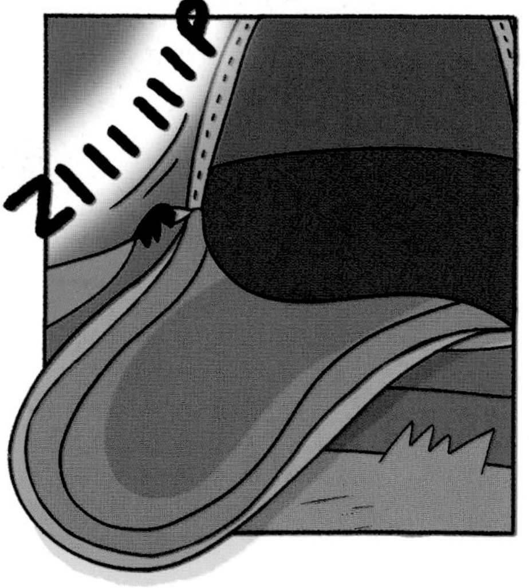
ZIIIIIIP

I'm good!
EASY TENT

??
DIRECTIONS

Need any help?
Nope!

I think I got it!

SNAP

I need help.

So what do we do after the tents?
Then we have lunch.

Great. I'm starving!
I could definitely go for some macaroni.
Or a pizza!
Or a cheeseburger with extra pickles, curly fries, and a strawberry milkshake!

We are having a toasty...
Roasty...
Delish-i-oasty...
Pot of beans!
BLUB
I think I'll just eat my pickles, thank you very much.
BLUB
BLUB

This has been the worst day of my life.

Have you ever had expectations shattered into a million pieces?

Well, I have and let me tell you something--

RIBBIT

BOING

SPLOOSH

MY PICKLES!!!

ALBERT!!!

ALBERT!
ALBERT!
ALBERT!
JOHN MUIR

Albert! Come quick!
My pickles are in THE MUD!

You smell like pickles...
And there's something on your butt.

Huh?

Ohmygosh.

AHHHHHHHHHHH!!!

GET IT OFF! GET IT OFF!
Stay still!

IT'S GONNA BITE ME!
IT'S GONNA BITE MY BUTT!!
Please don't bite my butt. Please don't bite my butt. Please don't bite my--

THWACK

EEP!

Pickles!
Are you all right?

Is it still there?

Yep.

AHH!!
WHAT IS IT?!

Is it rabid?
Oh yeah, it's rabid.

Just tell me when it's gone.
It's gone.

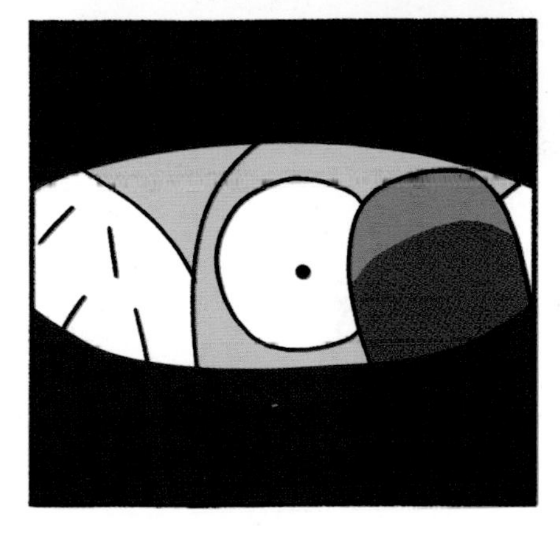

OH MY GOODNESS!
It's so cute!

Little tiny baby,
I love you...

Little tiny baby,
you know it's true.
WHOOSH

C'mon, Baby, let's go play.

I think we should try to find its mama.

But, Albert, I'm having so much fun.

I could be its mama. We look so much alike.

Pickles, how would you feel if YOU were a lost baby?

MAMAAA
toot

I guess you're right...
But how do we find her?
We look.

And if we don't find her,
then can I keep it?

Albert?
Then can I keep it?
Sure.

Mama Koalaaa?
Mama Koala?
Mama Koala, are you under there?
Run for your life!
Hellooo? Mama?
Z
Z
Z
ALBERT!!!

Mama Koala,
we found your baby.

DO NOT
DISTURB

I dunno, Albert,
I don't think the mama is here.

FUMP

I guess I have to
be your mama now.

There, there, Baby.

Mama.

Did you hear that, Albert?!
Baby Koala called me Mama!

Hey, look at this.
BEWARE
THE WOOLLY MOON BEAST
It's destiny!

BEWARE
THE WOOLLY
MOON BEAST
Beware the Woolly Moon Beast?
What's a Woolly Moon Beast?

I'm not sure.
Mama!

Baby koala, is this your mom?
Mama!
BEWARE

Maybe it calls everything Mama?

Okay, Baby, what's this?
Leef.

Flowr.

Stik.

Pebbul.
toot

clowd.

Owel.

BEWARE
THE WOOLLY
MOON BEAST
Mama!

Yep. That's its mama all right.
I bet this cave is close by.

C-C-C-CAVE?!

Albert, you know how I feel about caves!

The darkness...

And the cavey-ness...

It's scary.

How about you go look for the cave...

And we'll stay here on the stump of safety.

But what if I see something amazing? I'll be sad you're not with me.
There's nothing amazing about nature, Albert.

That's not true.
I can think of lots of things.

Like all the different trees.

And fungi.
And the pretty way the sun shines through the leaves.

To be in nature is a gift.

Well, I think it's something else.

Maybe you just haven't had your moment.

My moment?
Yeah, everyone has at least one special moment in nature.

A moment that makes you feel ALIVE.

How will I know if
I'm having my moment?

You'll just know.

I guess I see what you mean...

These flowers are nice.

And--
Shhh!

Did you say something?

I said SHHH!

Albert, the shrub is speaking.

I don't hear anything.

RUSTLE
RUSTLE

Platters!

I thought you went out for a steak?
What?

Oh my gosh, you came to rescue us!
SQUEEEEZE

Not exactly.

You smell like pickles. And you have a koala on your head.

That's Baby Koala. I'm its mama.

Just until we find its real mama. Have you heard of the--
Shh.

Quiet.
I'm on a secret stakeout mission for...

Whipser, whisper, whisper.

A spoon of yeast?
Monsoon treats?

A holiday feast!

BEWARE
THE WOOLLY MOON BEAST
THE WOOLLY MOON BEAST!!!

BEWARE
Oh yeah, we found one of those earlier.
Gasp!

MORE EVIDENCE!
BEWARE

Someone is trying to warn us...
CLICK
BEWARE

Because the legend is true.

Legend?

The Legend of the Woolly Moon Beast says a giant monster lives here.

Some say it has big claws...
SHING

Red glowing eyes...

And sharp teeth...

CHOMPING anyone who gets too close!

And I'm going to prove it's real.

But how can a scary monster be a mom to something so cute?

What do you mean?

Supposedly the Woolly Moon Beast is Baby Koala's mom.
BEWARE
THE WOOLLY MOON BEAST

Maybe the baby thinks everyone is it's mom?

Okay, Baby. Who am I?

Duhk.

What?! I'm not a DUCK. I'm a platypus!

Baby Koala, who's this?
Mama.
See?
BEWARE

And now we have to find the scary cave!

I'm secretly hoping we don't find it.

Oh, you mean that cave?
GO AWAY
DANGER
BEWARE
KEEP OUT
Gulp.

GO AWAY
DANGER
How do we get over there?
We need a plan.

OK, everyone, bring it in close.

That's too close.

Our mission is to get Baby Koala safely to the cave.

MISHN

BUT THERE COULD BE DANGER!
DANGER
DANGER
DANGER
DANGER

Gasp!

DANJR

So we make a slingshot to shoot the baby into the air and over the danger.

Platters, we can't throw a baby in the air.

Hmmm...

OK, new plan!

We dig a tunnel under the lake
right up the the cave on the other side.

It's genius.

I dunno...
There's gotta be an easier way.

Well, it's not
like a bridge will
magicaly appear.

Baby Koala, what is that?
BEEP
BEEP

BEEP
BEEP
BEEP
BEEP

Hey, do you hear that?
BLUB
BLUB
BLUB

It's a popping bubbly sound.
It wasn't me. If it was, you would know.
Hey, guys...

I think you might want to see this.

GO AWAY
DANGER
BEWARE
KEEP OUT
BLUB
BLUB
BLUB
BLUB

Hee-hee!
CLICK

A bridge!

This bridge was activated by the Mega Remote 2000. Very high-tech.
Where did you find that, Baby Koala?
GO AWAY
DANGER

I dunno, but I better keep it under here for evidence.

OK, team, camera's ready. Let's do this.

C'mon, Pickles.

PANT
PANT

Listen, Baby Koala, I want to help you. I do. It's just...

There could be ANYTHING under that bridge!

There could be ANYTHING in that cave!
RAWR!

I know you are just a baby and think the world is made of rainbows and candy, but it's scary out here.

Trust me...

And just because someone is older than you doesn't mean they aren't less afraid of things.
BOING
What I'm trying to say is...

I can't help you.

Baby Koala?

BABY KOALA!!!

??

Come back!
It's too dangerous!

Fwog!

Hi, Fwog.
PET
PET

I've had enough of you, Devil Frog.

You can take my pickles,
but you can never take my baby!

Oh, thank goodness...you're safe.

Now, you listen to me, buddy--

PLIP

Don't even think about it!

Baby Koala...I'm warning you.

I'll count to three and you back away from the edge.
One...two...

SPLASH
Whee!

GASP!

Guys! Help!!
Baby Koala jumped into the lake!!
OK. we need a plan!

THERE'S NO TIME FOR PLANS!

Albert!
Pull the tab on the back of my hat!
The what?

THE TAB!!!

I see it.
YANK

I'm going in.
Whoa.
CLICK

Could one of you maybe test the water first and tell me if it's cold?
Pickles! Hurry!

PLUNGE

Evening!

Baby?

Baby Koala,
are you in there?

Yes, my love!
I'm here!
Ahh!!

Hee-hee.

Baby Koala!

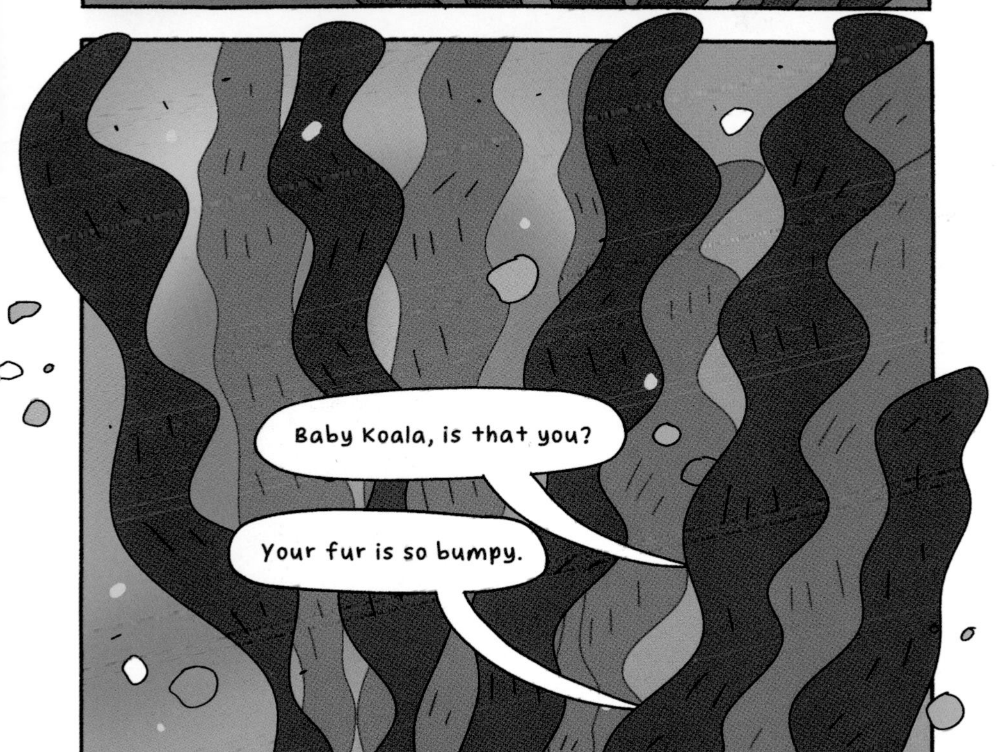
Baby Koala, is that you?
Your fur is so bumpy.

And your baby teeth are pointier than I imagined.

Not to make you feel bad or anything. I had a pointy tooth once. Just ask my mom, she--

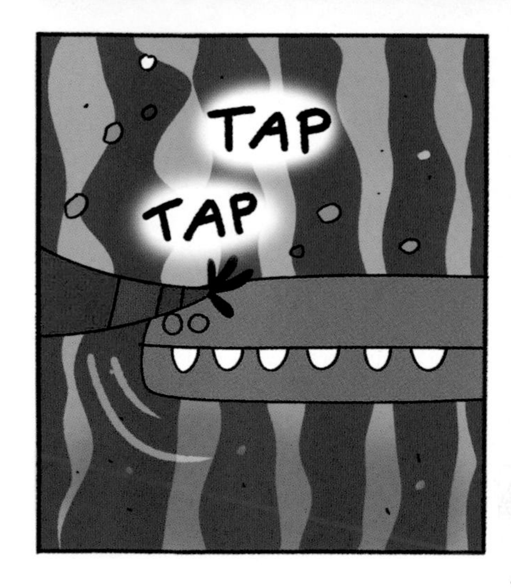
TAP
TAP

Ohmygosh.

AAHHHHHHHHHHHHHHHHHHHH!!!

HELP ME!!!
'Ello again!

Baby Koala! Grab my hand!

EVERYTHING IS GONNA BE OK!

Now GO!
Save yourself!
WHOOSH

Just promise to never forget meeeeee.

Ta-da!

Yeah!!
Wooo!!

That was AMAZING!!

I didn't know you were a crocodile tamer!

Oh...

I guess I am, huh?
CROC POWER

That was really brave.
It was EPIC!

What's it doing?
I think it wants a belly rub.

Umm...I'll pass for now.

And look!
You made it to the other side.
GO AWAY
BEWARE
KEEP OUT

Oh no, where's B--

Don't worry,
the little rascal is safe.
Hey, where'd you get that hat?
DANGER
BEWARE

From a catalog, where else?
Never know when you'll need
a safety suit.

Well, guys...I guess it's time...
GO AWAY
DANGER
BEWARE
KEEP OUT

Should we ring the doorbell?
GO AWAY
DANGER
BEWARE
KEEP OUT

Go ahead, crocodile tamer.
Go ahead, Albert.

How about whoever has the koala on their head has to ring the doorbell.

WHOOSH

No!
Baby Koala!

Go on Platters's head.

Hey, don't eat
my pom-pom.
Ow! My eyelids!
Stop smacking
my head!
SMACK
SMACK
The baby is hitting
the remote under your hat!
BEEP
BEEP
BEEP
SMACK
SMACK

Go AWAY
DANGER
Mama!
KEEP OUT

STOMP
STOMP
STOMP
Mama come nowww!

Mama.
Mama.
Mama.

YOU'RE the Woolly Moon Beast?!

GO AWAY
DANGER
BEWARE
Hello.

I see you made
some new friends.

And took Mummy's remote...
I was wondering who turned
on my cocoa machine.

DANGER
BEWARE
Sorry, he loves buttons.
We could tell.

And pickles.
SNIFF
SNIFF

AHHHHHHHHHH!!!
Yep.
That makes sense now.

Wait a minute, Mama--
Miss Moon--
Moon Mama--
You can just call me Sheila.

Sheila...

Why are you pretending to be a Woolly Moon Beast?
WARE
WOOLLY
ON BEAST

I waited in a shrub for FIVE HOURS!

The thing about koalas is...

We're exhausted!
Everyone is obsessed with how cute we are.
It's too much attention!
BEWARE THE Woolly MOON BEAST

I mean, LOOK AT US!
CUTENESS OVERLOAD

We can't catch a break.
Which is why I put up the signs...
BEWARE THE Woolly MOON BEAST

And the bridge...

And made a mixtape of monster noises.
STOMP STOMP STOMP
BOOGA BOOGA

Actually I sort of do sound like a monster.
Sorry if I scared you.

GO AWAY
DANGER
Would you like to come inside for some cocoa?
KEEP

WHAT?! YES!
MORE THAN ANYTHING IN THE ENTIRE WORLD!

Do you have marshmallows, Sheila?
Yes.
BEWARE

Wipe your feet!

Welcome to our home.

It's a luxury cabin.

With a cozy chair by the fire!

And books!
HISTORY OF PICKLES

And a pouf!

Over here is the indoor pool.

Jacuzzi...

BEEP
UNDER the stars.

COCOA XPRESS
K
And kitchen.
BEEP
BEEP

It's my dream come true!

It's so comfy.
We like comfort.
Would you like the massage on?
Massage?

T-h-i-s-s-s i-s-s-s a-a-a-w-e-s-o-m-m-m-e.
BEEP

Speaking of comfort, would you like to camp here tonight? We have extra blankets.

Well, this turned out GREAT, because I brought my snazzy bathing suit!

Albert, we don't have to stay if you don't want to.

I know you were excited about camping and the trees and the bright light that shines through the leaves.

True, but YOU went on an adventure with me. Crocodiles and all. And I couldn't be a prouder friend.

It's always an adventure with you, best friend.
BFF
BFF

Hold it right there!
Wait for us!

CLICK

Sorry it's not the picture you were hoping for, Platters.

That's OK. It's better.

HOME
SWEET
HOME
Hey, guys! I think it's starting.

Wowwwwwwwwwwwwwww.

Albert, I think I'm having my special moment now.
I knew you would.

The end.
RIBBIT

ABOUT THE AUTHOR

Maddie Frost is the (maybe-someday award-winning) author-illustrator of several picture books, like *Smug Seagull*, *Just Be Jelly*, *Wakey Birds*, *Capybara Is Friends with Everyone*, *Iguana Be a Dragon*, and more. This is her first graphic novel.

She is not a fan of camping.

Maddie lives in Massachusetts with her husband (who likes camping) and their two dogs (who also like camping).

Visit her online at maddie-frost.com.

BEANS